To Scout and Poppy
from their grandad

First published 1967 as *The Two Giants* by Brockhampton Press Ltd

This edition published 2014 by Walker Books Ltd, 87 Vauxhall Walk, London SE11 5HJ

2 4 6 8 10 9 7 5 3 1

Copyright © 1967, 2014 Michael Foreman

The right of Michael Foreman to be identified as author/illustrator of this work has been asserted by him in accordance with the Copyright, Designs and Patents Act 1988

This book has been typeset in ITC American Typewriter

Printed in China

British Library Cataloguing in Publication Data:
a catalogue record for this book is available from the British Library

ISBN 978-1-4063-5176-7

www.walker.co.uk

Two Giants

Michael Foreman

WALKER BOOKS
AND SUBSIDIARIES
LONDON · BOSTON · SYDNEY · AUCKLAND

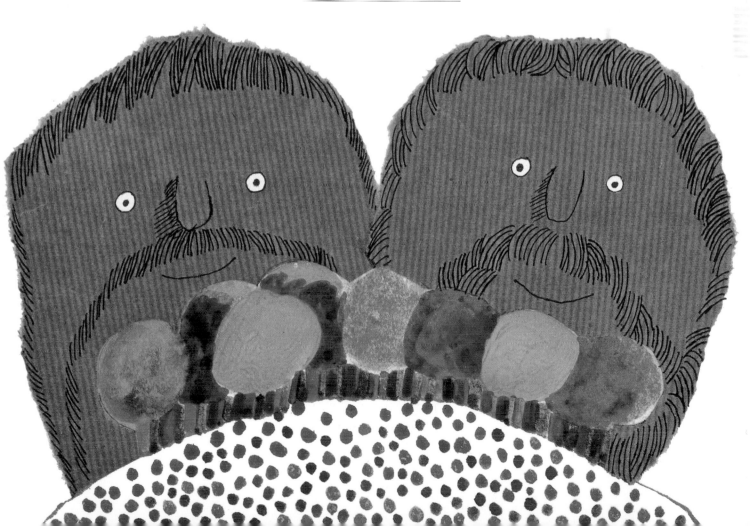

Once, long ago,

Two Giants lived in a beautiful country.
In summer it was warm, and in winter the land
was even more beautiful under snow.

Each day the Giants walked together among the
mountains and through the forests, taking care
not to step on the trees. Birds made nests in
their beards, and everywhere the Giants went,
thrushes and nightingales sang.

One day, while paddling in the sea, the Two Giants found a pink shell. The shell was very bright and both Giants admired it.

"It will look lovely on a string round my neck," said the Giant called Boris.

"Oh no! It will be on a string round <u>my</u> neck," said Sam, the other Giant, "and it will look better there."

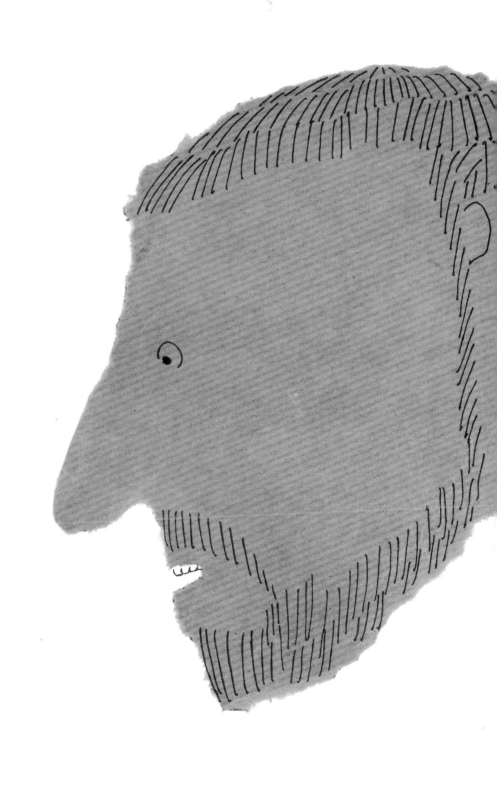

For the first time in their lives they began
to argue. And as they did the sun went
behind a cloud and the cloud became bigger
and blacker. The wind blew and blew and the

waves and clouds grew and grew. It began to
rain. The more the Giants argued, the colder
the day became. The waves swept higher and
higher up the beach.

Boris and Sam began hurriedly pulling on their socks.
Before they could put their shoes on, a huge wave
completely covered the beach.

The wave swept away the shoes and the shell.

The Giants were furious and threw stones at each other
as they ran towards the mountains to escape the flood.

Soon the whole country was covered by water except for the tops of two mountains, which became the only islands in a wide, cold sea. Boris lived in one and Sam in the other.

It was cold. They liked snow, but it never snowed. Winter followed winter. The Giants forgot how lovely the summers used to be. Each day was just dull and terribly cold.

They grew more angry than ever, and instead of stones they now threw huge rocks at each other.

On Mondays Sam would throw a rock at Boris.
On Tuesdays Boris would throw a rock at Sam.
On Wednesdays it was Sam's turn to throw
again, and so on, every day except Sundays,
every week.

After both Giants had been struck many times
on the ear and the nose and the tops of their
heads, their anger knew no limits.

The sea was dotted with rocks which the Giants had thrown, and one day Sam decided to use these rocks as giant stepping-stones. He waited until Boris was asleep, then picked up his huge stone club and climbed out of his mountain.

He planned to reach the other island, hit Boris on the head, and make him sleep all day and miss his turn to throw a rock.

Sam leapt onto the first rock. Then he leapt out onto the second rock.

As Sam reached the third rock, Boris

opened one giant eye. He saw Sam,

snatched his club, and whirling it round

his head, jumped out of his mountain and

began leaping from rock to rock towards

his enemy. The whole world shook

as the Two Giants charged

towards each other.

Suddenly both Giants stopped. Sam looked at the feet of Boris. Boris looked at the feet of Sam.

Each Giant had one black-and-white sock and one red-and-blue sock. They stared at their odd socks for a long time.

Gradually they remembered the day the sea had covered the land. In their haste to escape the flood, the Giants had got their socks mixed. Now they could not even remember what they had been fighting about. They could only recall the years they had been friends. They dropped their clubs into the sea, and laughed and danced. When they returned to their islands, each found a small white flower and felt the sun warm on his shoulders.

The sea began to recede.

Flowers grew where the water had been.

The birds returned to the islands.

Soon the two mountains were separated by nothing but a valley of trees. The country was large and beautiful once more. Sam and Boris sat among the flowers, and sometimes a grasshopper would jump

onto Sam's ear, or a butterfly would land on Boris's nose and birds would sit on the tops of their heads amidst the hair and flowers. The Giants were happy. The seasons came and went as before.

Sometimes the Giants strode about
their country, deep with grass or
leaves or snow. Sometimes they
made giant footprints in the sand
by the sea. Sometimes they just
lay in the woods which were full
of birds and marigolds.

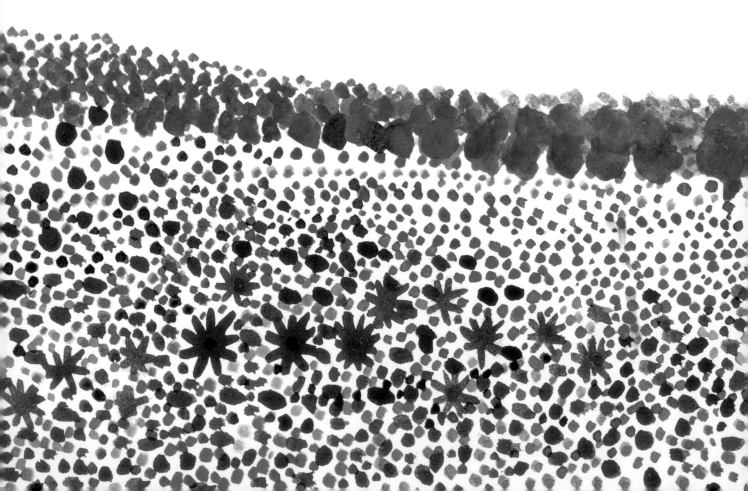

Whatever they did, they always wore odd socks.

Even when one of them had a new pair, he

always gave one sock to the other Giant ...

just in case!